DISNEY
PIRATES of the CARIBBEAN
—DEAD MAN'S CHEST—

THE CHASE IS ON

Adapted by Tennant Redbank

Based on the screenplay written by Ted Elliott & Terry Rossio

Based on characters created by Ted Elliott & Terry Rossio
and Stuart Beattie and Jay Wolpert

Based on Walt Disney's Pirates of the Caribbean

Produced by Jerry Bruckheimer

Directed by Gore Verbinski

Printed in United States of America
First Edition
1 3 5 7 9 10 8 6 4 2
Library of Congress Catalog Card Number: 2005934907
ISBN 1-4231-0089-1

DISNEY PRESS
New York

Captain Jack Sparrow was a lucky man. He had cheated death—many times.

After eleven years, he finally had his ship, the *Black Pearl*, back. But Jack Sparrow's luck had just run out.

Late one night, Bootstrap Bill
came to Jack. Bootstrap Bill
was the father of Will Turner.
But he was no longer human.
Starfish clung to his face.
"Davy Jones sent me. You made
a deal with him," Bill said.

This was not good news. "Any
idea when Jones will release
the beastie?" Jack asked. He
was talking about the Kraken,
a horrible sea monster. The
Kraken wanted to drag the
Pearl to the bottom of the
ocean. And Jack along with it!

"I told you, Jack. Your time is
up." Then Bootstrap Bill
pointed to Jack's hand. The
dreaded Black Spot appeared
there. Jack was a marked man.
Now the Kraken could find
him anywhere. Jack was no
longer safe on the water.

Meanwhile, in Port Royal, it was Will Turner's wedding day. But before he could marry Elizabeth Swann, soldiers ruined the wedding. They arrested both the bride and groom and threw them in jail.

Why were they in jail? Jack Sparrow. Jack had a Compass that the mean Lord Beckett wanted. To save Elizabeth, Will had to find Jack and get the Compass.

Will finally found Jack on *Isla de Pelegostos*. Jack did not want to leave dry land. He was still afraid of the Kraken. But things had suddenly gotten too hot for him on the island.

He needed to get away. With Will's help, Jack escaped the island. But now Will wanted Jack's Compass. It was the only way to save Elizabeth.

Jack had a plan. "I will trade you the Compass," he said, "for this." Jack pulled out a cloth. On it was a picture of a key that Davy Jones kept with him at all times. It was the key to Jones's heart.

Jones kept his still-beating heart locked away in a chest. Jack knew if he had the heart, he could get Jones to call off the Kraken.

Will agreed to the trade. He knew the trade would be the only way to keep Elizabeth safe.

Next, the *Pearl* found Davy Jones's ship, the *Flying Dutchman*. It was made of wood and bones and covered with shells and seaweed. Will went aboard.

Davy Jones looked as strange as his ship. One of his hands was a lobster claw. His beard was made of octopus tentacles. His crew was odd-looking, too. They had all sworn an oath to Jones.

Now Jones wanted Will to swear the oath. He wanted Will to be part of the crew . . . forever.

Will had other plans. "I challenge Davy Jones," he said. The game? Dice. The bet? "I wager my soul," Will vowed.

Davy Jones liked that offer. But if Will won, Jones had to give him the key. Jones scowled. A tentacle from his living beard pulled the key out. The key was hanging around his neck. That's all Will needed to know!

They rolled the dice. Then they bet. With help from Bootstrap Bill, Will did not lose. He would be allowed to leave at the next port. His father would not.

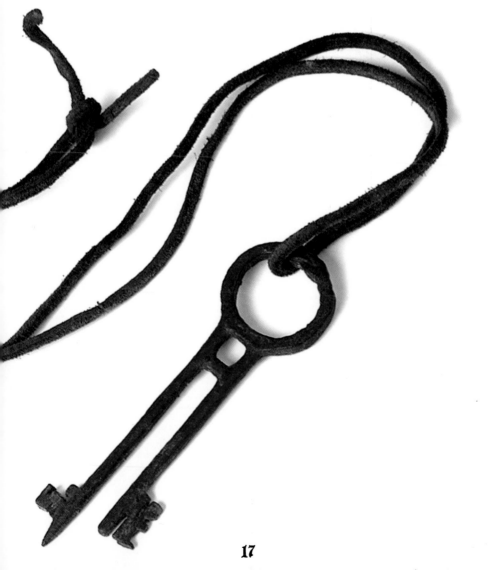

Later, while Jones slept,
Will stole the key to his chest.
Then he escaped from the
Flying Dutchman to another
ship. But Davy Jones soon
found out that the key was
gone. He sent the Kraken
after Will.

The monster broke the ship
Will was on in two. At the last
moment, Will grabbed onto
the *Flying Dutchman*. He clung
to its side. He would go
wherever it did.

And where was that? To *Isla Cruces*, the island where Davy Jones had buried his chest. The *Black Pearl* was also headed there.

While Will had been trying to save Elizabeth, she had gotten out of jail and tracked down Jack Sparrow. "All I want is to find Will," Elizabeth told Jack. Jack got excited when he heard these words.

He took out his Compass.
"This Compass points to what
you want most in the world,"
he said. So Elizabeth held the
Compass and the needle
swung. It pointed to *Isla
Cruces* . . . and Will.

Jack and Elizabeth set sail,
following the Compass.
When they got to the island,
they stopped. The Compass
pointed to a spot in the
jungle. It was where the chest
was buried. They started to
dig. *KONK!*

The shovel hit something.
A chest! Jack opened it. He
pulled out a smaller box. Jack
and Elizabeth put their ears
against it.

They heard a single, deep beat. "It's real," Elizabeth said. Now Jack just needed the key to open it.

Suddenly, there was a noise
behind them. Was it Davy
Jones? No. It was Will!
Elizabeth raced to him. But
Will was angry at Jack. Jack
had tricked him . . . again!
Now Will wanted the heart.
And Jack still needed the key
that Will had.

Jack and Will drew their swords. They started to fight! Their swords flashed. The key was swapped back and forth between them. Meanwhile, two other pirates made off with the chest! Elizabeth went after them. And then Jones's crew arrived and came after *them.*

For a moment, the chest was forgotten. But Jack got the key and left Will behind. He opened the chest. The heart! Jack put the heart in a jar filled with dirt. Then he, Will, and Elizabeth ran to the *Pearl*. As soon as they were aboard, the ship sailed.

"We are in no danger," Elizabeth said. Wrong! Suddenly the *Flying Dutchman* shot up out of the sea right in front of them! The *Black Pearl* rolled. Jack dropped the jar. It broke. The heart wasn't there. It was gone . . . and so was Jack's safety.

Now, no one on the *Pearl* was safe. The Kraken had come for Jack. The pirates loaded the cannons and fired. The Kraken was hit! It pulled away. "It will be back!" Will said. "Abandon ship!" Jack yelled. Will went to the rowboat. Elizabeth and Jack stayed behind. She chained Jack to the mast. "The Kraken's after you," Elizabeth told him. "It's the only way."

Jack nodded. "Pirate," he called her. That should have been an insult, but not to Jack. To him that was high praise. Elizabeth jumped into the rowboat.

The Kraken returned.
"Hello, beastie," Jack greeted
the monster. The Kraken
wrapped its long arms
around the *Pearl* and pulled
the ship down into the sea.

Was it the end of Jack Sparrow? No one knew for sure. After all, Jack Sparrow was a lucky man. He had cheated death before. Perhaps he could do it again!